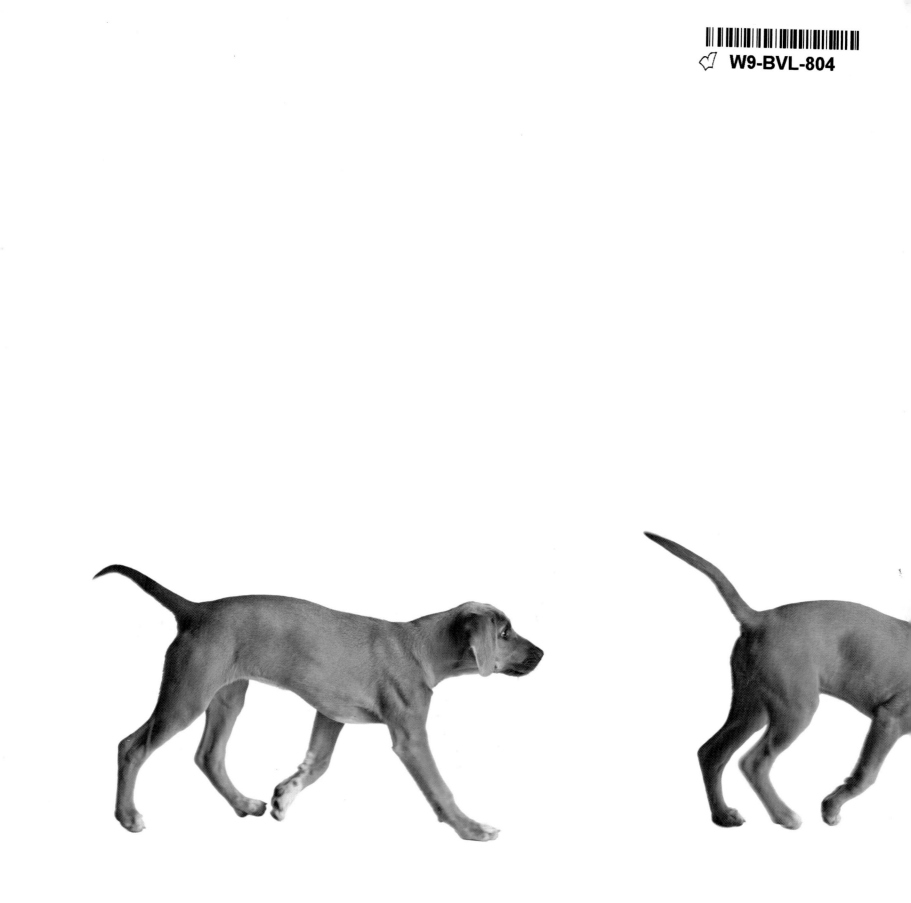

A Home for Dixie

The True Story of a Rescued Puppy

by Emma Jackson

with full-color photographs by Bob Carey

Collins

An Imprint of HarperCollins Publishers

For Thalia Zarokyan,
my inspiration for life
—E.J.

Once upon a time, there were

three puppies. One was red, the second was brown, and the third was brown with a black nose and white paws. They were sisters, but they didn't have a mother or a father, and they didn't have a home. The puppies were all alone and needed to find help very soon.

Just in time, a dog rescuer named Mary Cody heard about the puppies and made up her mind to help them. But by the time the puppies got to Aunt Mary's Doghouse, they were very sick. The tiny brown puppy with the black nose and white paws was the sickest of all. Aunt Mary took her to the dog hospital right away. She would need to stay there for a while, but Aunt Mary knew she would get better.

Sure enough, the puppies got better, and soon they were strong enough to take a look around. Aunt Mary's Doghouse was filled with dogs! Big dogs, little dogs, healthy dogs, hurt dogs, old dogs, and young dogs. All the dogs had been rescued and all were hoping to find a new home.

Meanwhile, not so very far away lived a girl named Emma. For as long as she could remember, Emma had wanted a dog. Almost every day she asked her parents, "Can we get a dog? Can we please get a dog? Can we pretty, pretty please get a dog?"

Most of the time, the answer was no.
Once the answer was "Let's get a fish,"
so Emma got a fish named Mariko.

Once it was "Let's get a
hamster" (named Pixie).

Finally it was "Let's get a
guinea pig" (Wilbur).

Emma loved all these pets, but they were *not* the same as having a dog.

Then one day Emma asked again, "Can we please get a dog?" and the answer was yes!

Emma thought they would go right to a pet store and come home with a puppy. But her dad said first they needed to find out as much as they could about getting a dog. Emma and her parents checked the internet, and soon they found a website for Aunt Mary's Doghouse. It seemed like the perfect place to look for her dog.

And that is how Emma learned that there are millions of dogs living in animal shelters, abandoned or turned in by owners who can't take care of them anymore. They don't have homes or families. Emma knew that somewhere out there was a homeless dog waiting just for her.

At the Doghouse, a visit from a family is a very big deal. The puppies in the puppy area were so excited. "People! People!" The sisters hopped up and down. "Could these be my people? Could this be my family?"

Emma sat down on the floor, and the puppy that was brown with a black nose and white paws jumped into her lap and looked up at her. This puppy was the one!

Aunt Mary said that they needed to choose a name.
Emma's mom liked Dixie, because the puppies were
found in South Carolina, and Dixie is sometimes used as
a nickname for the South. Emma's dad is from the South,
so he liked it too. And Emma liked it because Dixie is a
cute name, and her new puppy was very cute.

Aunt Mary told Emma and her parents to go home and talk about their decision to adopt Dixie. It was very important to be absolutely one hundred percent sure they were making the right choice.

Emma was sure. They called Aunt Mary the next day, and soon they were back to pick up their puppy. Aunt Mary packed Dixie's toy lion and her squeaky parrot in a box and hugged and kissed the puppy she had rescued.

Dixie said good-bye, and off she went with her new family.

Home at last!

For Dixie, this new home was a palace. There were three brand-new laps to sit on, more toys than she had ever seen, lots of treats (Emma's mom even baked homemade dog biscuits!), and a fluffy pink bed just for her.

The first day was truly wonderful. But then came the first night.

It was awfully dark. And very quiet. Dixie was all by herself in her crate in the kitchen.

She started to cry. And she couldn't stop. Whimper. Whimper! Dixie got louder and louder.

Emma sat up in her bed. Had she made a big mistake? Was having a dog too much responsibility for her after all?

She got out her sleeping bag, carried it into the kitchen, and lay down next to her new puppy.

By morning, they both knew it was settled. From now on, they would take care of each other.

Sometimes Dixie does things she's not supposed to, like chewing sneakers. Sometimes Emma gets so busy with sports and homework that she doesn't have that much time to play. Or she doesn't feel like going out for one more walk. But Dixie and Emma always forgive each other, because they are very best friends.

This is how Emma takes care of Dixie.

This is how Dixie takes care of Emma.

Emma is proud that her family adopted a dog that needed a home so badly. At first, she thought that they were giving Dixie a new life. But Dixie has given something wonderful to her family, too. Emma and Dixie both know that they will be best friends forever.

Do you think you're ready for a new best friend? Dixie's two sisters have already found loving homes, but there are many more wonderful dogs like Dixie available from **Aunt Mary's Doghouse** and hundreds of other rescue groups and shelters across the country.

A great place to start your search is www.petfinder.com. Petfinder can help you:

•Learn what's involved in adopting a pet from a shelter or rescue group—what to know before you go look and what kinds of questions to ask.

•Understand what's really involved in taking care of a pet, from commitment to cost.

•Make a great match by searching more than nine thousand animal shelters and rescue groups across the United States, Canada, and Mexico for a pet best suited for your household.

•Find volunteer opportunities at shelters or rescue groups in your vicinity.

If you're looking for a dog and live in the NJ, NY, PA, CT area, check out Aunt Mary's Doghouse at www.AuntMarysDoghouse.com.

AUNT MARYS
DOG HOUSE

Aunt Mary's Doghouse is a nonprofit charity made up of Mary Cody and a small group of dedicated volunteers. What makes Aunt Mary's Doghouse unique is that they save the dogs almost no one else will. They get dogs from overcrowded shelters or they rescue dogs in trouble from the streets. Hundreds of dogs considered unadoptable have been saved and placed in loving homes, thanks to Mary's efforts. The American Red Cross awarded Mary its Bravo for Bravery medal for 2007 for her tremendous accomplishments in animal rescue.

A portion of the proceeds from the sale of this book
will be donated to AuntMarysDoghouse.com.

Collins is an imprint of HarperCollins Publishers.

A Home for Dixie

Text copyright © 2008 by Emma Jackson

Photographs copyright © 2008 by Bob Carey

Special thanks to Mary Cody for the photograph on page 8.

Manufactured in China.

www.harpercollinschildrens.com

Library of Congress Cataloging-in-Publication Data is available.

ISBN 978-0-06-144962-8 (trade bdg.) — ISBN 978-0-06-144963-5 (lib. bdg.)

Design by Rachel Zegar

1 2 3 4 5 6 7 8 9 10

❖

First Edition